EGMONT

EGMONT
We bring stories to life

First published in Great Britain in 2020 by
Egmont Books

An imprint of HarperCollins*Publishers*
1 London Bridge Street
London SE1 9GF

www.egmontbooks.co.uk

Written by Matt Yeo
Edited by Katrina Pallant
Illustrated by AndoTwin, Moreno Chiacchiera (Beehive Illustration) and Sean Longcroft
Designed by Grant Kempster, Cloud King Creative

This book is an original creation by Egmont Books

Text and illustrations © Egmont Books 2020

ISBN 978 1 4052 9896 4
71142/004
Printed in Italy

CONTENTS

MEET THE FARTERS!

Look out for these six chuffing characters in each busy scene. In each case, can you work out which one of them is actively causing a stink? See below the other pongy items to spot in each scene. All the answers are at the back of the book, along with some bonus items to locate.

FLATULENT FLAMINGO

This cool bird likes nothing more than chilling out and letting rip. This feathered farter attends all the best parties and she certainly makes an impact with the terrible toots trumpeting from her rear!

UPWIND UNICORN

This rare magical creature is often found hiding in the most unusual of places. If her sparkly coat and flowing mane weren't enough to make her stand out, her super stinks are the stuff of legends.

SIR STINK-A-SLOTH

Elegant, sophisticated and mild-mannered, this furry fellow also tends to break wind at the drop of his hat. He usually spends his time hanging around half asleep, pumping out particularly pongy parps!

4

ROBO-TRUMP 2000

The ROBO-TRUMP 2000 is the ultimate in bottom burping technology. Able to pass gas at the speed of sound, this mucky mechanical marvel's futuristic farts are so powerful that they can sometimes be seen from space!

FARTY FRENCHIE

Bonjour, from this hairy honking hound! He may look super-cute but wherever he goes in the world, this parping pup smells so bad that he's often mistaken for a stinky skunk.

NIFFY NARWHAL

What a pong! Even the salty sea can't wash away the stink of this whiffy whale. Unlike his fellow narwhals, this particular pumper prefers to spend his time on dry land, leaving terrible trumps behind.

BONUS ITEMS!

As well as the six main characters, can you find all of these non-farting items hidden in each stinky scene?

TEST YOUR STINK– FINDING SKILLS

We've taken it easy on you for this first smelly search. It's not too tricky to find the farty friends, but how quickly can you find the stinky decoys? Don't get too comfortable though, the rest of the book is much more challenging!

TRUMPY THEME PARK

It's a family fun day out at the theme park! One of the farters has already started smelling the place out. Sir Stink-a-Sloth is hanging with his mates and Upwind Unicorn is eating as much candy floss as she can!

FIND THE FAKE NARWHAL

FIND THE DECOY ROBOT #2

15

WHIFFY WATER PARK

Are you ready to get wet and wild? Slip and slide you way around the wackiest water park in the world. Niffy Narwhal's looking to make a splash, but why did he have to eat that chilli burrito for lunch? PAARRRPPP!

FIND THE FAKE FLAMINGO #1

WAFTING WINTER WONDERLAND

There's nothing better than hitting the slopes on a fresh, crisp winter morning! But will the temperature take a tumble now that Farty Frenchie and his foul friends are here to parp up the place?

FIND THE DECOY DONKEY

FIND THE
FAKE
UNICORN

STINKY SKATE PARK

It's a busy day at the skate park and everyone's showing off their skills. Keep an eye out for BMX riders, skateboarders and scooter riders doing all the latest tricks. Sir Stink-a-Sloth wants a go too, but his terrible toots might knock him off balance!

FIND THE FAKE FLAMINGO #2

23

HONKING HOLLYWOOD MOVIE SET

Lights, camera, FARTING! A major motion picture studio sound stage is always a busy place, filming everything from sci-fi epics and wild westerns to soppy romances, but it will feel like a horror show when someone drops a big stink!